Story by Lore Segal · Pictures by James Marshall

ALL THE WAY HOME

A Sunburst Book
Michael di Capua Books
Farrar, Straus and Giroux

For Annie and for Julia
L.S.

For Victoria Frese
J.M.

Copyright © 1973 by Lore Segal
Pictures copyright © 1973 by James Marshall
All rights reserved
Library of Congress catalog card number: 73-82699
Published in Canada by Collins Publishers, Toronto
Printed in Singapore
First edition, 1973
Sunburst edition, 1988

Once upon a time there was a mother

and she had a little girl whose name was Juliet and
a baby called George and she took them to the park.

Juliet fell down.

Juliet closed both her eyes and opened her mouth as wide as she could and howled.

Her mother kissed her. "Did that make it better?" the mother asked Juliet.

"Whaaa," answered Juliet, "it's all better now."

"So what are you crying for?" asked the mother.

"Because I feel like it," howled Juliet. "Whaaa!"

"And what are you grinning at, George?" asked the mother. "Stop it, both of you. All right then! We're going home this minute!"

"All right," hollered Juliet, "then I'm going to cry all the way."

So they were walking along, the mother, and Juliet crying "Whaaa," and George grinning...

when they met a dog.

The dog said, "What's the matter with Juliet? Why is she making so much noise?"

"Dog," said the mother, "I don't know, and she's going to do it all the way home."

"Well then, I'll tell you what I'll do," said the dog.

"I'll walk behind Juliet and I'll close both my eyes and open my snout as wide as I can and I'll bark all the way home."

So they were walking along, the mother, and Juliet crying "Whaaa," with George grinning and the dog barking...

when they met a cat.

The cat said, "What ever is the matter with Juliet and that dog? Why are they making such a lot of noise?"

"Cat," said the mother, "I wish I knew, and they are going to do it all the way home."

"Then I'll tell you what I'll do," said the cat.

"I'll walk behind the dog and I'll close both my eyes and open my mouth as wide as I can and I'll miaow all the way home."

So they were walking along, the mother, and Juliet crying "Whaaa," with George grinning and the dog barking and the cat miaowing...

when they met a bird.

The bird said, "What on earth is the matter with Juliet, and the dog and the cat? Why are they making such a racket?"

"Awful, isn't it?" said the mother.

"I'll tell you what I'll do," said the bird.

"Let me guess," said the mother. "You'll walk behind the cat and close both your eyes and open your beak as wide as you can and you'll squawk all the way home?"

"Right!" said the bird.

So they were walking along, the mother, and Juliet crying "Whaaa," with George grinning and the dog barking and the cat miaowing and the bird squawking...

when they came to the house where Juliet lived.

The doorman stood in the door. He shook his head and said, "Uh-uh! You can't come in here, not with all the noise you're making!"

So they had to go on walking, the mother, and Juliet crying "Whaaa," with George grinning and the dog barking and the cat miaowing and the bird squawking, past Juliet's house and up the street and around the corner and around the next corner and the next corner and the next, and when they got back to the house where Juliet lived...

the doorman stood in the door and shook his head
and said, "Uh-uh," so they had to keep walking on,
the mother and Juliet and George and the dog
and the cat and the bird, crying and grinning and
barking and miaowing and squawking.

And as they were turning the corner before the house where Juliet lived, she closed her mouth and opened both her eyes and said, "Mommy, I have to whisper."

Juliet's mother bent her head down. "I don't feel like crying any more. I want to go home," Juliet whispered. Then Juliet's mother whispered in Juliet's ear and in George's ear, and George stopped grinning.

When they got to the house, the doorman quickly
opened the door and Juliet and George and the mother
ran inside. But the dog and the cat and the bird with
their six eyes closed, and one snout, one mouth, and
one beak barking, miaowing, and squawking,
walked right past and up the street.

If you see them coming round the corner, tell them to stop making such a racket because Juliet isn't crying any more.